VELVET SKY, ARIZONA

THE TRAVELER #2

J.C. HULSEY

DEDICATION

To my lovely wife of over 50 years for her encouragement for my attempting this project.

ACKNOWLEDGMENTS

To Google, for being my spell checker, my thesaurus, my all-around information center.

To Amazon, for allowing me to publish my books. To my Dell computer, who has been my constant companion both day and night and to my Kindle Fire HDX that I have with me constantly.

For all those authors, whose books I have enjoyed reading through the years and have been inspired by them to finally try my hand at writing a book?

CHAPTER ONE

Orville, Half Loaf, and myself, were on our way to Velvet Sky, Arizona Territories. We decided to go there when I remembered Pa telling me that he had a younger brother living there. He said there were four brothers that came by wagon train from Chicago, ranging from seventeen to twenty in age.

They were of Irish descent. Their Pa and Ma had passed on, and there was nothing to keep them in Chicago. My pa, being the oldest, was supposed to make the decisions for them. James Seamus was the second born, then Francis Leroy, and Justin Lucas was the youngest.

When they passed through the Texas Panhandle, they decided to part ways because of the tension that was building between them. They weren't happy with the decisions Pa was making, so Pa decided to head to South Texas, where he heard there was a need for a good Blacksmith. They said their goodbyes and Pa headed south, then the three remaining brothers headed west to California.

Pa found out later that James had stopped in a little settlement called Velvet Sky, in the Arizona Territories. According to the correspondence he had received, Uncle James had a big cattle spread situated in a valley below the Mountain Range, just east of Velvet Sky.

Orville said, "I think we should stop in the next town to get this buckboard checked over and have it repaired, as it's needed for a trip like this. And, maybe, we should consider getting another horse to help Whitey (the Palomino that he bought from Senor Murrieta at his Rancho in South Texas) pull the wagon. Maybe I'll trade that no-good saddle that I thought I was going to use." (He had traded for a saddle when we were at Trader Tom's Trading Post.)

"That all sounds good to me. How about us finding a spot to camp for the night?"

Orville said, "I've always wanted to see how them cowpokes rope those cows and brand 'em."

Half Loaf said, "I am ready to travel, just to see this beautiful and wonderful country of yours."

As I looked at the countryside, I couldn't understand Half Loaf's description. There were sporadic tufts of trees, on-again, off-again grasses, and shrubs as far as the eye could see. It was a surface that looked as hard as stone, and even less inviting.

"I reckon we need to check our supplies and head that direction," I exclaimed.

CHAPTER TWO

Suddenly, a windstorm blew up and dust was everywhere—on leaves, branches, even on my teeth and lips. Then, just as suddenly, it stopped, and in the distance, I saw what looked like an oasis, a green strip of thick grass that carpeted the narrow strip along its length. Cottonwood trees had sprung up; young trees, little more than twice a man's height.

What a welcome sight, after just experiencing a dust storm. I waved to my comrades and pointed to the green strip ahead. We all headed toward it, and the air turned cooler as we got closer.

"Almost feels like winter, don't it?" Orville exclaimed. We all jumped down and ran to the banks of the little spring, falling down and placing our faces into the water to drink our fill. What a glorious, cool, sweet-tasting refreshment it was. When my thirst was slightly quenched, I rose and told the guys we needed to water the animals.

Orville unhitched Whitey. Half Loaf and me led our horses, along with Orville, to the little stream and let them drink their fill. As they were drinking, I stood in awe at the miracle that God had created. Such a wonderful paradise in the middle of this vast dry land. It looked as if the stream just bubbled out of the ground, rushed along for about fifty yards, and then disappeared back into the ground.

Half Loaf suggested that we set up camp and enjoy this wonderful wet place, take baths, and wash our clothes . . . especially Orville. Orville said he couldn't help it if he sweated more than most folks; it was something he inherited from his daddy's side of the family.

We enjoyed the rest of the day swimming and splashing in the cool water, and then we washed our dirty clothes. When we had hung all the wet clothes on the low branches of the trees, we started a fire and cooked something to eat.

Orville boiled some rice and fried up some Prairie Hens that he shot this morning, then mixed them together for a superb meal, with rice pudding for dessert, and a fresh pot of hot coffee. It was a delicious meal; one fit for a King.

Half Loaf cleaned the dishes and put them away. We all helped set up the tent, then unrolled our bedrolls and bedded down for the night. When I finished saying a prayer, Half Loaf said, "I would like to know this God with whom you talk."

"I will be glad to introduce Him to you. Do you believe the Bible is the Word of God?"

"Se, Yes, I believe it to be true."

"The Word of God tells us in Romans 3:10 'As it is written, There is none righteous, no, not one . . . ' That means I'm not righteous, you're not righteous, no one is righteous. Then it says in Romans 3:23, 'For all have sinned, and come short of the glory of God.'

"That means I have sinned, you have sinned, everyone has sinned. Then in Romans 6:23, 'For the wages of sin is death; but the gift of God is eternal life through Jesus Christ our Lord.' Because we are all sinners, we deserve to die, But God said we don't have to die, if we accept the gift He has for us.

"Romans 5:8-9, 'But God commendeth (that means gives proof of) His love toward us, in that, while we were yet sinners, Christ died for us.' God gave his only Son so that we would not have to die but have everlasting life. Salvation cannot be earned. Everyone is a sinner and deserves death, but God gives eternal life if we accept Jesus Christ as our Saviour. All you have to do is tell

God that you are a sinner and you want to accept Jesus as your Savior."

"Yes, I wish to do that."

"Just bow your head and ask God to save you."

Half Loaf did just that, and that night another soul's name was added to The Book of Life.

Not only did we get to enjoy this beautiful, green pasture that God created, but we also had the privilege of showing someone the way into heaven. *Isn't it a wonder the way God weaves people into our lives?*

It was a restful night. I slept soundly, and woke the next morning refreshed, ready to leave.

We enjoyed warmed-up supper that was left over from last night, then cleaned the dishes.

We stowed the tent in the wagon and headed toward the next town, which was about fifty miles due east.

CHAPTER THREE

After two days of traveling, I pulled up on Sugar's reins and stared at the trail ahead, then turned in the saddle and looked at the dusty trail behind. It looked like silver water running off a duck's back, and the land in front of us seemed to sizzle, like a burning flame. Some of the terrain looked vaguely familiar, but upon looking a second time, it didn't look like anything I had seen before. As I took yet another look, the subtle rise and fall of the land all looked the same. The temperature hadn't changed one degree in the last six hours, and there was no wind blowing, except a slight breeze every half hour or so.

It seemed as if the wind might be hiding just over the next rise, waiting to surprise us. Then as we rode over that next rise, there always seemed to be another rise hiding the wind. I lifted my eyes toward the west, where the ground was bathed in a purple gray and the sun was ever receding behind the horizon, then turned and waved for Orville and Half Loaf to follow in that direction. We traveled for another hour and a half, then stopped under some giant oak trees to rest.

We tethered the horses to some low-hanging branches, and Half Loaf brought two buckets of water over to let two of the horses drink their fill. Then he allowed the other two to drink. Orville had gathered firewood and had a campfire going in no time at all, while I started getting the cooking pots and set them over by the fire, then I went back to the wagon and retrieved the tripod to hang the pot over the fire. As soon as Orville had the fire going, he started peeling some spuds.

Just then we heard two shots. Orville ducked behind the wagon, and I fell to the ground right where I was standing. Half Loaf came walking into camp, talking really fast in Mexican, with his head hanging.

"What's wrong Half Loaf?" I asked.

"I saw a couple of rabbits and tried to shoot them for our meal, but I missed and they ran off," he answered.

Orville said, "We gotta teach this kid how to shoot, and shoot straight."

"I am ready to learn now," replied Half Loaf.

"Let's have something to eat first, and then we'll have your first lesson," I told him.

After we finished with the meal, I went with Half Loaf some distance beyond the camp.

"First of all, we're not gonna try to teach you any fast draw stuff, or anything like that. We just want you to shoot straight," I told him.

We shot at targets until we ran out of cartridges for his pistol. "We will have to replenish your supply at the next town," I told him.

When we got back to camp, Orville was mixing up a batch of biscuits. He added a little more flour to the ingredients and stirred vigorously. He didn't make biscuits very often, but when he did, they were the flakiest I'd ever tasted.

He placed the last biscuit into the Dutch oven. "Half a dozen is all we get tonight, cause we're completely out of flour. We sure need to find a town or settlement real soon. Flour's not the only thing we're running short of.

I watched him mix the batter, then pinch off a portion of dough, flatten it, and place it into the Dutch oven resting over the fire. The aroma was heavenly, and it caused my stomach to growl.

He said, "Better grab a plate and dish up some of those spuds and beans, these biscuits will be ready in just a bit."

"Do you think we should give him the special thing we have for him?" asked Half Loaf.

"What special thing are you talking about?" I asked.

Orville spoke up. "When we took those varmints' guns and stuff to the mercantile back there in Angel Falls, he had something new. He said it came all the way from Chicago. Something he called a tin can. And listen to this, there's peaches in that can. Yep, peaches. That the special something I told you I got for you."

"How do we get those peaches out of that can?" I asked.

"It just so happens, the storekeeper had something called a can opener, so I got one of them, too," Orville said.

Minutes later, we sat enjoying the fire's warmth and the quietness of the night, eating beans and taters with flaky biscuits, and washing it down with water from the canteen. It was a simple meal, but quite enjoyable.

We were all amazed at the tin can, especially when Orville used the can opener. There were four peach halves inside the can.

"Since these are a special treat for you, Jed, you can have two peaches."

When I finished with the peaches, I looked across the fire at the faces of my two friends; their tanned faces were glowing like shining bronze.

I laid the tin plate aside and exclaimed, "That is the best special gift I have ever received. Thank you very much, both of you."

After the dishes were cleaned and put away, we rolled out our bedrolls and hunkered down for the night. I lay my head on my pallet, rolled onto my back, and stared up into the night sky, letting my eyes wander from star to star, then said a prayer for the fantastic friends that God allowed to come into my life.

I rolled back onto my side as I felt the weariness of the day creeping into my bones, and closed my eyes as darkness enveloped me. The next thing I knew, I was looking into the sun, thinking how it resembled a sparkling jewel on the bosom of the hard-packed earth ahead.

CHAPTER FOUR

We loaded up, saddled our mounts, and headed due east. As we crossed from Texas into New Mexico Territory, we came to a town called Windy Butte. It was a real metropolis, when compared to the places we had been. We went straight down Main Street and stopped at the livery stable near the end of town. I noticed that the streets were empty, not a soul to be seen.

Most of the businesses were locked up. The saloon, however, the fourth building down from the livery stable, was open and very loud.

We stopped in front of the Livery Stable, then the door opened and a little man wearing an old miner's cap, leather trousers, and a green shirt, stuck his head out and said, "Let me open the big door and you can bring your animals inside."

"Where's all the people?" I asked the old timer.

"Everybody's locked up tight, afraid to show their faces, afraid of gittin' killed," he answered.

"Can you, maybe, expand on that just a little," I asked.

"Well, you see, it's them, Swearinger brothers, Clem and Clyde. They is the most vicious men I've ever seen. Clyde worships his big brother and hangs on his every word, and is more than willing to join him in whatever evil deed Clem is attempting. Three days ago, they robbed and killed a man and his wife, took the little ten-year-old daughter out to the barn and had their way with her, then they strung her up and slit her throat. As they left, they torched the house and ran off all the stock. A most horrendous act that needed to be answered for. They rode into town, big as you please, on two big stallions, prancing down Main Street, and tied up in front of the saloon.

"They strode in laughing loudly and bragging about how the little girl screamed. There're still over there in the Saloon drinking and laughing and bragging. Something needs to be done, but the sheriff is hiding out in his office afraid to face them."

"You're right about one thing, Old Timer."

"Yeah, what's that?"

"I reckon if nobody's gonna step up and do this job, then I guess it's up to me to git it done"

"Orville said, "You don't have to do this Jed, it's not your responsibility."

"If not me, then WHO?" I turned into the street and walked toward the saloon, removing the tie down from the hammer of my pistol. I stood out in the middle of the street in front of the saloon. The boardwalk was littered with empty bottles and crumpled trash. Tinny piano music drifted through the doorway, and the sickening smell of liquor assaulted my nostrils.

I hollered for the two men who were inside celebrating to come outside.

A couple minutes passed, then the door of the saloon opened slowly and two men stepped out onto the boardwalk. One to the left side of the door weighed 180 pounds. He was five nine, with a broad, round face, pleasant features, and brown skin tanned by the sun. His eyes were blue and very expressive, and he had broad white teeth, a square, brawny form, though well proportioned, with every muscle fully developed.

The other one stopped just outside the door. He was a medium-sized, toe-headed sort of a man, with liquid blue eyes, and a mouth that stretched nearly ear to ear. His face was as smooth as a baby's bottom, and didn't have a particle of hair on it. He walked with a shuffling, half-apologetic sort of a gait, and had a squeaking, boyish voice, with awkward, gawky manners.

"What'cha want Kid? You the one doing all that caterwauling out here?" he screeched.

"First of all, I don't like to be called Kid. Secondly, you can do me a favor. Come with me to the Sheriff's Office to confess your sins and be locked up, or if you prefer, I will introduce you to the devil and you can confess to him."

"I ain't going no place with the likes of you. Better step aside, or I'll walk right over you."

"Like I said, and I'm asking nicely, come along and everything will turn out alright."

He looked at me as if I were invisible and, at that moment, I saw his eye twitch just a tad. I drew and fired, just as his gun cleared his holster, and he was slammed backward through the saloon door as the bullet entered his chest, just above his heart.

His brother threw his weapon into the street and raised his hands in surrender.

"I didn't do nothing. Honest. He was the one did it all. I didn't do nothing," he exclaimed.

I suggested to Clyde that he mount up and ride out of town without looking back, and that is exactly what he did, leaving his pistol lying where he had thrown it.

I was replacing the spent cartridge when I spotted the Sheriff headed toward me. I was just holstering my pistol when he asked, "What happened here? Who are you, and who is that man?" He pointed at the dead man.

The town suddenly came to life. Doors started slamming, and folks started gathering around making a lot of noise.

"I asked you a question, kid," said the sheriff again.

"I wish people would stop calling me that," I said softly.

"What's that, speak up boy," said the sheriff

"My name is Jed Jenkins. Me and my friends just arrived in town a little while ago. When I heard of the Devil's spawn running loose in this town, I decided something needed to be done, so I did it," I answered.

"Devil's what? What is it you're saying? Did you shoot that fellow, or not?"

"I was doing what nobody had the nerve to do, and that includes the Sheriff of this town."

This evil deed was committed by these two men, and I just couldn't let them get away with it, especially when no one was stepping up to correct this wrong. The owner of the livery stable told me what these men had done, and how they was bragging about over in the saloon. So, yes, I did shoot him," I answered.

"Maybe you better come with me back to my office and let's see if there's a flyer on you."

"Sure thing, Sheriff. I wouldn't want to do anything wrong, or to upset you in any way whatever. After you, I'll follow."

"Charlie, you and some men, clean up this mess."

CHAPTER FIVE

I fell in behind the Sheriff and marveled at how he was able to stand up straight, let alone walk. He was probably six feet tall, and had a head that looked as big as a watermelon; it looked too big for his skinny body. He weighed in at maybe 110 pounds, with a pockmarked face, long, stringy hair hanging to his collar, and he wore a big, ten-gallon hat with a crown that hadn't been shaped yet. His double holster setup looked to weigh as much as he did.

We reached the jai, and he motioned for me to go ahead of him, so I stepped into the well-lit room. It had windows all along the front wall, and there was a wooden rail fence separating the entrance from the main office, which held a desk and two file cabinets. There was a rifle rack beside the door to the cells in the back, and the desk was a big mess with papers strewn across the top. I turned to face the Sheriff, and found myself looking straight into the barrel of a Colt .45.

"What's the meaning, Sheriff?" I asked.

"I think you'd better unbuckle your sidearm, place it on the desk, then open that door and step into one of the cells while I look over these posters to see if you're wanted anywhere."

"You're making a mistake, Sheriff," I told him.

"I think you're just trying to cover your unwillingness to act by blaming someone for something, anything to make yourself feel useful. You know I did you a service by eliminating that scum for what they did to that family, especially for that little, innocent, ten-year-old girl, and maybe, just maybe, saving your life in the process."

He lowered his weapon, hung his head and said, slightly above a whisper, as he glanced up at me with his smoky gray eyes, "I didn't want to be Sheriff, it was forced on me by the Mayor and his cronies. He owns most of the businesses in town, including the Saloon, which was my downfall. I gambled too much, lost more than I could afford, and the only way I could square up with him was to take this job and do what he told me to do. I didn't realize at the time that the deck was stacked and the dealer was crooked as a snake. There was no way I was gonna win.

"Then he took my place as collateral. I had worked for five years for it, and was just starting to pay it off when this happened. I'm not a gunman, I'm a farmer, and that's what I wish I could do. My name's Jackson Hadley. Me, my wife, and my boy are living in the Sheriff's little house behind the office. It consists of two very small rooms. Let me tell you, my wife is one very unhappy woman. Whenever I would lose at gambling, I would sell off the livestock, then all my tools. Finally, all that was left was the homestead. It was like a disease with no cure. No matter how hard I tried, I couldn't stop. But, you know, since I've been sheriff, I haven't gambled any at all. Funny, ain't it, now with nothing to lose, I don't have no desire for it."

"Maybe there is a way. Why don't you just have a seat and wait for me to check into this matter. I'll let you know something real soon."

"You would do that for me, someone you don't even know?" he asked.

"I feel that God has ordained a certain path that He wants me to follow, and when He places a person in that path that needs help, I feel obligated to do the best I can to help them. I feel that you are one of those people," I answered. "You sit tight and I will get back to you as soon as I take care of a few things."

CHAPTER SIX

I left his office and went to the telegraph office to send a wire to the bank in Angel Falls, Texas. I asked them to convey to the bank here in town that I needed some money, and to transfer it from my account. I had just left the telegraph office when a group of men came up to me.

The finest-dressed man stepped forward and extended his hand said, "I'm Colonel Beauregard T. Madison, the mayor of this fine town, and we have proposition we would like to discuss with you. Could you please follow us to my office just up the street here?"

"Sure, I've got a few minutes to spare, lead the way," I said.

We walked past the businesses, and I noticed that most of them had the name Madison on them. Exactly as the Livery Stable owner had told us. When we reached his office, he turned, said, "Thank you gentlemen, that will be all, please return to your duties. Would you please come inside?" he asked me.

"This is my brother, Theodore. He helps out with my business ventures. I don't know what I would do without him."

A young girl came bursting through the back door. "Daddy, Daddy! Oh, I'm so sorry, Daddy, I didn't know you were in a meeting. I'll come back a little later."

"That's okay, Baby, let's go in the back room and you can tell me what it is that you want."

"I apologize, Sir. This is my daughter, Melody Susan Madison. Now if you will excuse me, I will return shortly."

Theodore stood and said, "I don't know what he wants you to do, but whatever it is, you need to leave as fast as you can. I assure you; he is up to no good."

"I appreciate the warning, but I need to see this through to the end, whatever that might be."

"Don't say I didn't warn you. Whatever happens, my hands are clean."

"My brother was in the Army alright, but he sure as heck weren't no Colonel. He was a Corporal. It makes him feel important when they call him Colonel. Me and Beauregard made it through without injury, mainly because we served in Headquarters. I was a General's clerk, and Beau was in the General's private mess detail.

That's as close as either one of us got to a Colonel. I take care of his legitimate dealings. I refuse to get involved in the shady ones."

The back door opened and the Mayor came back inside. "Now where were we? Ah, yes, I was about to offer you the job as Sheriff of our fine town."

"I thought you already had a sheriff, one of your choosing, if my information is correct."

"Yes, I'm sad to say. He was indeed my choice, but as you have probably noticed, he's just not up to the task. What do you say, will you accept the position? I can assure you; it is a very lucrative position for the right person."

"Don't you think I'm a little young for the job? What will folks say about someone so young being the Sheriff?"

"I believe most folks in town saw what transpired between you and the Swearinger brothers, and how it turned out. Besides, if anyone questions you, I have no doubt whatsoever that you are capable of handling it."

"I don't know, Mayor. I need time to talk it over with my partners. May I give you an answer in, perhaps, two or three days?"

"Fine! Fine! I'm sure you will make the right decision. Please come by the office here and let Theodore know what you decide. Theodore has consumption, and is not able to do any strenuous work. We moved here to the

Arizona Territories because of Theodore's illness. He inherited this little plot of land just outside of town from our grandfather right after the war ended. Grandfather didn't live very long after the war. He was very upset because the South surrendered. He was too old to serve, but he saw to it that his sons and grandsons served.

"The Madison's used to own the largest Plantation in Virginia. Grandfather won this plot of land in a poker game. After the war ended, there wasn't much left of the Plantation, and father and our two Uncles lost their lives. Now that I think about it, perhaps it would be better if you will accept an invitation to come to supper at my house Saturday night. My house is located at the end of Main Street. It's the brick one with the white picket fence. The bricks were shipped from back east, by a freight company located right here in our town. Say seven o'clock? You can give me your answer then."

CHAPTER SEVEN

The Livery Stable owner inspected the buckboard and determined that it needed more repair than he could accomplish. He did, however, have a buckboard in the back of the Livery Stable that he bought from a family that had left for greener pastures, as they had put it.

"Orville asked, "What do you gents think about a new wagon?"

Half Loaf said, "We will need another horse, because the wagon is bigger. It will take two horses to pull it."

"Just so happens I have something to address that problem, follow me gents." He walked out in back of the stable. In the corral were four horses milling around, each vying for attention. There were two Grade Horses that looked really good, and two big Morgan horses, one a tan gelding, and the other a brown stallion. They were all fine-looking horses. The tan gelding pranced and whinnied more so than the other three, so Orville walked over to him and rubbed the white tuft between his eyes.

Orville waved me off to the side. "I figure if we got the stallion, he'd be on the prod for every mare we come across. Better we settle on the tan gelding, won't have to worry 'bout him none."

Orville winked at me, then said to the owner, "I reckon how much you got to have for this broken-down horse and that broken-down buckboard?"

I grinned at the way Orville described the horse and wagon that he and I both knew we were going to buy.

"What do you mean? You know that that is the finest animal in the bunch and, as far as the wagon goes, you also know it's in tip top shape," answered the owner.

"No need to fuss. How much, taking my old buckboard in trade?" Orville asked. "I also got a real good saddle to throw in this little transaction."

"Well, I really don't have no use for your wagon, other than for spare parts, but I'll make you a mighty fine deal," replied the owner. "I'll let you have the wagon and the gelding for the fair price of $200."

"We'll give $150.00 and throw in the saddle," I said.

"Sounds like we made a trade." The owner nodded.

Half Loaf and me loaded all our goods from the old wagon into the new one, while Orville brought the gelding from the corral in the back.

We had to swap out harnesses, because we now had two horses to hitch to the buckboard. That cost us another thirty dollars that we really couldn't afford.

"I'm going to have to send a telegram to the bank at home and ask for more money," I said.

"Maybe we can find some work here in this town they call Windy Butte. Why you think they call it that?" inquired Half Loaf.

The old timer said, "Probably 'cause back in '61, there was a big tornado came whistling through, right down the middle of Main Street. Didn't tear down no buildings, 'cause it blew just on that street. Only stirred up a powerful bunch of dust. Reckon that's why."

Orville and Half Loaf headed out of town to set up camp, while I went to the mayor's house for dinner.

CHAPTER EIGHT

The dinner was superb. After we ate, the mayor asked me into the drawing room. "Have you reached a decision?" he asked.

"I really don't believe I'm suitable to be wearing a badge, and besides, my partners and I are on our way to the Arizona Territories, to a place called Velvet Sky. My Uncle has a cattle ranch there. I do appreciate your offer, but I must decline. Surely, you can find a suitable candidate here in Windy Butte. There is, however, something you could do for me. You could give the sheriff back his land. You could do this as a favor to me. It makes me very happy when people do favors for me. On the other hand, I tend to get unhappy when I ask for a favor, nicely, and nothing gets done. I asked the Swearinger brothers to do me a favor, they refused."

"Yes, yes, I see what you mean. I believe we can grant you that little favor. I was just telling Theodore that Hadley had been sheriff long enough, and earned enough to pay off his debt. I will have Theodore tell Hadley first thing in the morning. Is there anything else that I might do for you?"

"No, I believe that is everything. Thank you so much for dinner, and for offering me the job. Good night, sir. Please tell your lovely wife and daughter goodnight from me."

CHAPTER NINE

I stepped onto the porch, and was almost to the picket fence when I heard something in the bushes to the side of the house.

I reached for my pistol and, as I turned toward the noise, I saw Melody waving to me, so I walked over to her.

"I'm so glad I caught you," she exclaimed.

"What is it that I can do for you?"

"You have to help me. I'm trapped in this awful town. Will you help me?" She batted her eyes at me.

Her skin had an olive tint. Her eyes were light, creamy amber, with red-brown flecks, and she had dark-brown shoulder-length hair.

"I don't really see how I can help you."

"You need to talk to your father and explain to him how you're feeling. I'm sure he will do something."

"Yes, he'll do something alright. He'll lock me in my room and throw away the key."

"I think you're being a little overly dramatic. Surely, your own father wouldn't do that."

"You just don't know him. I told him about a young boy that wanted to come calling on me, and he talked to the boy's father and told him to keep his boy away from his daughter."

"I think all fathers are protective of their daughters, especially when they're the only child. How about your mother. Can't she help?"

"She does everything he tells her to do. Won't you please help me?"

"Since your father and I have an understanding, I'll talk to him on your behalf. Would that be satisfactory?"

"Oh, thank you so much. I just know he will listen to you. May I give you a thank you kiss?"

"I don't mind if you do."

She stood on her toes and kissed me on the cheek. "Thank you again. I will never forget you." She slipped back around the corner of the house.

I turned, stepped through the gate, climbed into the saddle, and headed for camp.

33

CHAPTER TEN

Orville had set up the tent just east of town, on a little knoll with a Mulberry tree standing alone at the top. They were both asleep when I arrived, so I didn't say anything to wake them.

The next morning, I awoke before they did. Usually Orville was awake first and had breakfast started. When he awoke, I asked him how he would like to have breakfast in town.

"That sounds like a winner. Let's wake Half Loaf and skedaddle. It will be something to eat somebody else's cooking. Don't happen often enough."

We saddled up and headed for town. The only eating place in town was located off Main Street on Bounty Street. We tied the horses out front, stepped up on the boardwalk, and headed in. We took the table on the right side of the room, and I sat with my back to the wall.

A pretty young girl with light, pale-green eyes, and blonde hair, came to the table and asked, "What can I get for you? The special today is pork chops, with brown gravy, with green beans and potatoes."

"That sounds fine, we'll all have that."

"What will you have to drink?" she asked. "We have iced tea, lemonade, or coffee."

"How on earth can you have iced tea in this hot weather?" asked Orville.

"We have ice shipped in from Boston, by rail, from Mr. Tudor, known all over as the 'Ice King,'" she answered.

"Well, let us have some of that ice tea," said Orville.

She was back in a little while with three tall glasses full of ice and a dark liquid.

"Say, that ain't bad," said Orville.

"What do you think, Half Loaf," I asked.

"It has a bitter taste. I do not like it."

Just then the waitress brought our meal. "I overheard what you said about the tea being bitter. If you add some sugar to it, I'm sure you will like it better," she explained.

Half Loaf turned the sugar jar upside down and dumped the whole thing into his glass.

"Oh no," shouted the waitress. "Just put two spoons in one glass. Here, I will bring you another."

"Thank you, Senorita," Half Loaf said.

We finished our meal and Orville said, "I think I'll have me just one more glass of that there iced tea."

When the waitress brought it, and Half Loaf asked her what her name was.

"My name is Polly Graham. I was born here in Windy Butte, but I hope to go to New York someday and sing in the big Opera House there."

"I also like to sing," said Half Loaf. "Perhaps we could meet tonight when your work is finished."

"I will be finished around six o'clock."

"I will see you then," said Half Loaf.

CHAPTER ELEVEN

We left the eating place and walked up the street to the General Store. It was large, dark and gloomy, and it had more merchandise than any of the other places we'd visited. The store clerk was completely bald, had bushy mutton-chop sideburns (they extend to the edge of the mouth and are connected to a mustache with no chin hair), and wore wire-rimmed eyeglasses. He was very thin, short in stature, and seemed extremely agitated when he spoke—not exactly the personality you would expect in someone who had to deal with people all the time.

We browsed for a while, and Orville gave a list to the clerk. "Can you have this filled by dark?"

The clerk perused the list. It included coffee beans, a new coffee grinder, assorted spices, baking powder, oatmeal, flour, cornmeal, salt, sugar, dried fruit, canned fruit and vegetables, honey and molasses, crackers, cheese, dried beans, salt pork, bacon, vinegar, a new Dutch oven, two new wooden buckets, potatoes, dried beans, chili powder, tomato sauce, soap, one special smoked ham, a lantern, coal oil for the lantern, and new dungarees and underwear for me and Half Loaf. It also included a new hat for Half Loaf, and four boxes of .36 caliber ammunition for Half Loaf's gun.

"I believe I can fill this without any problem. Haven't had an order this large in some time. I should have it ready by six o'clock."

"We'll be back," said Orville.

CHAPTER TWELVE

We left and headed back to camp, then I stopped and said, "Wait a minute. How would you fellows like to sleep in a real bed tonight?"

"That sounds like a fine idea," exclaimed Half Loaf. "I do have to meet with Polly for a little while, and then I would like very much to sleep in a real bed."

"That's fine, we'll meet you at the hotel directly across from the telegraph office," I told him. "Shall we say eight o'clock?"

"Orville and me will pick up our supplies and meet you there," I told him.

"I think the first meal I'm gonna fix is Range Riders Stew. I haven't had it in quite a while," Orville said.

Ingredients:

*1/2 lb. green cooking Apples

*5 Tbsp. Butter

*3/4 lb. Beef already cooked

*1/2 cup bread crumbs

*A dash of Nutmeg

*1/4 lb. Onions, sliced

*pinch Salt

*3 lbs. cooked sliced Potatoes

* Dash of Pepper

We picked up the supplies and loaded them into the buckboard, when Orville said, "I think I'll pass on the hotel. I got so used to sleeping on the ground in the Army that I don't think I could be comfortable."

"OK, if that's how you feel, we will see you back at the camp in the morning," I told him.

CHAPTER THIRTEEN

The next morning, after we had breakfast, we packed up. I told them I had to run an errand, then left for the mayor's office in hopes of persuading him to allow his daughter more freedom.

"There is one thing that we need to have an understanding about. I would sure hate to hear that my favor, which you said you would do for me, had been left undone. That would upset me in the worst way. I just might have to stop what I am doing and return to Windy Butte."

After our talk, I felt certain that things would be better in the Madison household.

When I got back to camp, everything was ready, so we headed out. That night, after camp was set up, Orville decided to make use of some of our new supplies. He took out the makings for cornbread. Using the new bowl, he poured the batter into our new cast iron skillet, then covered it with the lid. In a little while, he bent to check the coffee, then lifted the lid on the cast iron skillet.

The corn bread was golden brown and crusty, just the way I liked it. He opened some canned tomatoes and stirred them into a can of beans in a smaller skillet.

"I sure am glad that general store had all these canned goods," he exclaimed. (The farmer's wives had sold the canned vegetables to the store.) Of course, even though it's getting colder, we'll still have to use them up plenty fast, or they'll spoil.

I also bought us a smoked ham. I thought we would like it better than beans and bacon all the time," he said.

We dished up our meal and sat down to enjoy it.

"I have another surprise," exclaimed Orville. "Honey, to go on the cornbread. I always did have a sweet tooth."

What a meal! Of all the meals Orville had cooked, this was one of the best.

After the dishes and pots and pans were washed, we sat by the fire watching the flames. They flickered lower and lower, until there was nothing but glowing embers. The moon was very bright tonight. It resembled a sparkling jewel on the bosom of the hard-packed dirt. We said goodnight, and each headed to our beds.

I awoke early, estimating at least a half hour before the sun would crest the horizon, and felt a nagging sensation that something was wrong. Gray twilight masked the area straight ahead.

CHAPTER FOURTEEN

I saddled Sugar and went in that direction.

After about two miles, there was a dried-out creek bed, rutted with some deep gullies. There were a lot of rocks and boulders lying all around, and it looked like we might have trouble getting the buckboard across. I scanned in both directions, but this looked to be the best place to cross, as the creek bed got deeper and wider in both directions. I went back to inform Orville and Half Loaf of our problem.

"I knew I should'a got rid of that blamed wagon when I had the chance," he grumbled.

"If we had gotten rid of the wagon, we wouldn't have all these fine meals you've been fixing," I explained to him.

"I reckon you're right about that," he answered.

"What'd you reckon we're gonna do about that wash?" he asked.

"We'll work through it when we get there," I answered.

When we got to the creek bed, Orville said, "I recall a time just about like this in the Army, when we had to cross a big gully with the Mess Wagon. We moved all the rocks and boulders, and filled the ruts with them. Rolled right over the top of them, like it was a real road."

"Sounds like a plan to me. However, there is one thing. I want Half Loaf to wear a pair of the gloves that we bought back in town. I don't want him to get blisters the way he did when we chopped all that wood," I said.

"Let's have a quick cup of cold coffee and git started."

When we moved all the rocks and placed them in the ruts, we drove the wagon across, just like Orville said we could.

I wiped the moisture from my forehead with my bandana, drank deeply from my canteen, then poured a little into my hand and dabbed water on my face and neck. It sure felt good. I suggested we stop for a while, rest the horses and ourselves, then continue on.

CHAPTER FIFTEEN

"We might as well eat a plate full of cold beans and cornbread," Orville said. "There is also something else I've been thinking on. Since the weather is gittin' cooler, the dampness seems to creep into my bones while lying on the cold ground. I thought I might make me a pallet in the back of the wagon. I'm not gittin any younger, you know. I spent many nights on the cold ground when I was in the Army, but I was a lot younger then. I jest can't do it no more."

"Whatever you what to do Orville. It's okay with us."

"There was still plenty of daylight, so we loaded up and headed out. I stared off in the distance and saw scattered mesquite trees and the scarce, dry, distorted Tobosa grass. There was also tall, treelike cacti scattered as far as we could see. It was a dry land to be sure. I looked further to my left and spotted smoke curling into the clear sky, probably a mile and a half away. It wasn't drifting at all, as there was no wind. I waved to the guys and we headed toward the smoke. It took about an hour to arrive at a small farmhouse.

47

CHAPTER SIXTEEN

It was a clapboard frame two-room house. The yard was hard dirt, packed down from the horses and other animals. It was also hard, since there hadn't been any rain in a very long time. There was a thin elderly woman with gray hair hanging wash on the corral fence. A gray-haired man was just coming out of the barn. He looked up and saw us, then ran back into the barn.

He returned with his carbine, cocked and ready. "Stop right where you are," he hollered.

I raised my hands and said, "We want no trouble. We're just travel weary and wanted some friendly talk with someone other than each other."

"Forgive my rudeness. Man can't be too careful. Step down, come on in for a cup of coffee. Name's is Nolan Grigsby. I'll git the old woman to fix some victuals for ye, if yer a mind to join us for supper," he said.

"We'd be mighty proud to join you," I said.

"Mind if we water the horses?" I asked.

"You'll have to fetch water from that barrel over yonder. Please go sparingly, though. That's all we got till I go over to the neighbors for more. Our well went dry nigh on five days ago. If'n we don't git some rain, I don't know what we'll do," he said.

"How many barrels do you have?" I asked.

"Got four, but I kin only carry two in my wagon," he answered.

"Well, we can carry two in our wagon, and that will hold you twice as long," I told him.

"I'd be beholden to ye, if'n ye'd do that. Thanks."

"How far to your neighbor's place?" I asked.

"I reckon it's about twelve miles or so, too far to go today. We kin go in the morning, if ye've a mind to," he said.

"That sounds like a plan. Do you mind if we put our horses in your barn, maybe feed a little grain and brush 'em down? They don't get a lot of that out on the trail," I said.

"Help yerselves, grains a little short, so use it . . . "

"I know, use it sparingly." I finished for him. We took the animals into the barn. It was really run down.

"Looks like these folks need more than a little rain to fix them up. After we haul the water tomorrow, we'll see if there is anything else we can do to help them," I said.

"Come on in when yer finished, coffees on the stove," said the man.

We finished up in the barn, used a little water on our bandanas to wipe the trail dust off, and went inside.

"Have a seat there at the table. I already set the cups. All I have to do is fill 'em up," he said.

The lady of the house was busy stoking the fire of the old cast iron stove. She went to the counter and started peeling potatoes. When they were ready, she placed them in a skillet. As soon as they were brown, she put them in with some beans that were already cooked.

I thought to myself, *Beans and taters again!* But then why was I complaining? These good folks were willing to share what little they had with us, and us being strangers.

After we had eaten, Orville said, "Excuse me a minute. I need to get something from my wagon." He returned in a couple of minutes with a jar of berry jam and a slab of bread.

"I thought we would share a little treat with you fine folks after that great meal you fed us," explained Orville.

I looked at the lady, and she was dabbing her eyes with her handkerchief. "We ain't had nothing sweet in, let's see, it must be over two years," she said.

"I noticed, when we was in the barn, that you've got a cow. Is she fresh? Is she giving milk right now?" asked Orville.

"Sure is. She gives a gallon each day. Morning and night. She gives too much for the two of us. I give the extra to our two hogs. Sometimes I think they eat better'n us. The old woman used to make butter, but the churn got broke, and we ain't been able to replace it," he said. "Times have been mighty hard around here. Why you asking?"

"Well, I figured in the morning we might have us some hot cocoa. That is if everybody would like some."

"My, you boys is gonna spoil us with all these surprises. I've never had hot cocoa. What is it?" she asked.

"Wait till the morning, and you'll be even more surprised. I know it's something you'll like," Orville said.

"It's time to turn in, fellows. Let's go on out to the wagon and set up the tent. Goodnight, folks, and thank you for such a fine supper," I said.

CHAPTER SEVENTEEN

The next morning, we were up early. Orville took one of our buckets, milked the cow, then took it inside and asked Mrs. Grigsby if she'd mind if he fixed breakfast.

She said, "No not at all."

He went back to the wagon and brought in all sorts of victuals. "I think it's almost Thanksgiving. How about hot cakes, oatmeal laced with honey, and hot cocoa? For dinner, smoked ham, green beans, and boiled potatoes."

"That all sounds heavenly," she exclaimed. "Don't that sound heavenly Nolan?" She looked at her husband.

CHAPTER EIGHTEEN

After breakfast, we loaded the water barrels into both the wagons, and took off to the man's neighbor. It took almost an hour to reach his place. We reined up the horses and climbed down from the wagons.

A man stepped out of the barn and walked toward us. "Howdy, Grigsby, I see you're back for more water. My well is getting a little low, so I can't let you have as much as you been gittin'," he said.

"I sure appreciate whatcha been doing fer us, Pike, but if we don't get water, we just may have to move on," said Grigsby.

"Maybe we can reach some kind if agreement to satisfy everyone," I said. "How about if we pay for the water?" I asked.

"Well, let me think on that a little. I reckon if you could pay a dollar a barrel, I could live with that,"

"Let's fill 'em up!" shouted Orville.

I gave Mr. Pike four silver dollars, which he quickly stuffed into his pocket. We filled all four barrels and started back to Grigsby's place.

"I don't know how I'm gonna be able to repay you. I don't have a penny to my name. Haven't had none fer a year or so," he said.

"Don't trouble yourself about that. Just be thankful for what you receive, as if it's a gift from God."

When we arrived back at the farm, Mr. Grigsby said," I don't know how we're gonna unload those barrels from the wagons. They're mighty heavy."

CHAPTER NINETEEN

"That ain't gonna be a problem. We unloaded barrels such as this all the time in the Army," Orville said. "Do you have lids for these?" he asked.

"Sure, they're out in the barn," answered Mr. Grigsby.

"How 'bout you and Half Loaf go and git'em?"

They brought four lids back and handed them up to Orville, and he fastened two of the lids to the barrels in our wagon.

"Unless you think you'll be needing your wagon afore the barrels are empty, we'll leave those two in your wagon," he said.

"I don't reckon I'll be needing it before the barrels are empty," he said.

"Now, let's find two long poles to roll these barrels down onto the ground," said Orville.

There were some poles out behind the barn that Mr. Grigsby was going to use to build a pole shed.

"These will do just fine," said Orville.

We carried the poles back to the wagon, leaned them against the ground, and let them down onto the bed of the wagon.

"OK, now let's tip this barrel onto its side and roll it down. Slow and easy," Orville said

We got both barrels down without any mishaps, and set them next to the house so Mrs. Grigsby would be able to get water without having to travel too far.

Orville said, "Half Loaf, tote me two buckets of that new water into the kitchen. It's time I got busy cooking that Thanksgiving dinner that I promised."

Mrs. Grigsby had fresh coffee for us when we walked into the kitchen. She also had a couple cups of that hot cocoa, if anyone wanted it.

We finished the coffee and then Mr. Grigsby, Half Loaf, and me went outside. Mostly to get out of Orville's way.

"I was wondering if there were any chores that you haven't had time to finish up," I asked.

"Sure, there's a heap of things needs fixin', but I wouldn't ask you fellows to do my work for me," Mr. Grigsby answered.

"I don't mean to insult you, but I don't recall you asking us," I said.

We worked until a little after noon, when Mrs. Grigsby came to the door and yelled, "Come and git it."

We washed up using just a tad of water, because this was going to have to last for a while.

We went inside, and everything smelled delicious.

Orville had really fixed a spread for us. We all sat down, bowed our heads, and asked God for His blessings for this meal, and for these fine folks who He had led us to.

We finished the meal, then sat around visiting and listening to Orville's and Half Loaf's tall tells. Even though Half Loaf was a lot younger than Orville, he had some stories that would rival those of Orville. We had leftovers for a late supper, then we went out to the wagon to settle in for the night.

"I reckon we orta think about leaving in the morning," said Orville.

CHAPTER TWENTY

The next morning, we told the Grigsby's we were leaving.

Mr. Grigsby said, "I noticed you could use a cover fer your buckboard. I just happen to have one that we used when we came from Nebraska. It has the hoops and canvas that turn your buckboard into a covered wagon. If you think you could use it, I'd be proud to git it fer you."

"I sure would like it. Thanks a lot," exclaimed Orville.

Mr. Grigsby went to the barn and returned with a large canvas. "How about letting Half Loaf come with me to get the hoops?" he asked.

They returned with four wooden hoops. Mr. Grigsby showed Orville how to put them on the wagon and, sure enough, it looked just like a small covered wagon.

"This is just what I've been needing, especially since I'm gonna start sleeping in the wagon," said Orville.

When we were all packed and ready to leave, I asked the Grigsby's if they would pray with us. We all bowed our heads, and I asked the Lord to watch over and bless the Grigsby's. I then asked that He guide us along the trail that He wanted us to travel and bless us all.

"And one last thing, Mr. Grigsby, here's four dollars to get more water."

"Thank' ye so much. Go with God."

CHAPTER TWENTY ONE

We mounted up, waved goodbye, and took out toward the northeast, heading for the Arizona Territory.

We crossed from New Mexico into Arizona, and the land changed from open prairie to a mountainous range. To our rear, there was nothing but prairie grass gleaming golden brown as far as the eye could see. In front there were tall mountains with snow-tipped peaks. The weather seemed to change, and there was a brisk cold breeze blowing down off the mountain tops. We put our jackets on. From what I had heard, Velvet Sky was about four days ride from where we were.

CHAPTER TWENTY TWO

The scenery was so much different from what we had seen in Texas and New Mexico. It was open, as far as the eye could see. There was a lot of open range, but it was surrounded by mountains. Big, tall, snow-tipped mountains. I had to admit, it was beautiful.

The horse's hooves and wheels of the buckboard failed to disturb the hard-packed road that seemed to stretch all the way to the mountains.

After three days of traveling with nothing out of the ordinary happening, we saw what looked to be settlement in the distance. It was getting close to dusk, so Orville suggested we make camp, and go into town first thing in the morning.

The next morning, I stared at the halo of orange left by the Sun as it peeked over the horizon. We mounted up and rode into town. There was a sign with VELVET SKY painted on it, about ten feet from the buildings. The town itself was quite a surprise.

Other than the weather-beaten buildings, there was nothing but purple-hued mountains on the horizon. The town was little more than a whistle stop.

A few false-fronted buildings lined the narrow dirt road, with just a small boardwalk between. There were handwritten signs that declared CLOSED on all the buildings, even the barber shop and the saloon.

I didn't see any movement whatsoever, not even a dog, so we moved up Main Street to the livery stable.

It was closed, so Orville brought the wagon to a stop in front of it, set the brake, and hollered, "Yo! Anybody in there? If yer in there, we got some horses needs tending.

"Half Loaf said, "I will get down and knock on the door. Perhaps they are gone like everyone else." He dismounted, banged on the door.

"Who is it?" someone inside hollered.

"We just got into town and our horses need feed and shelter," I answered.

"Jest a minute," came the reply. The door opened and a man peeked out. "OK, come on in. I can help you," he said.

"What's going on? Why's everything closed? Did somebody important die?" I asked.

"Nope, Quince 'Black Patch' Forrest is in town."

"And who is Quince 'Black Patch' Forrest?" I asked.

"He's just about the meanest, orneriest polecat in five counties, that's who he is! He killed our sheriff a week ago. He's been running roughshod over town ever since. Ain't you never heard of him?" he asked.

"You say he's in town now. And that's why all the businesses are closed?" I asked.

"That's why," he exclaimed.

"Where might this fellow be right now?" I asked.

"That's him, yonder, by the saloon!" He ducked back inside as they looked.

"I reckon I'd better have a talk with this fellow."

"Now why you wanna go messing in other folks' business?" Orville asked.

"Like I've said in the past, if I don't do it, then who will?" I asked him.

I stepped into the hard-packed dirt road and started walking toward the saloon. I was about twenty feet from the saloon, when this rough-looking man stepped down off the boardwalk. He was dressed in a black shirt and trousers, had shoulder-length black, greasy hair, a thin crooked mustache, pockmarked face, and a patch over his left eye.

"Where you think yer going kid?" he scoffed.

"I understand you've been a bad boy," I said.

"I don't know what yer talking 'bout."

"I heard you killed the sheriff."

"Could be. What's it to you?"

"I reckon you and me need to go over to the jail and set you up with accommodations."

"Acomma what?"

"There's a cell in the jail that has your name on it."

"No man who walks this old earth, can tell me what to do!" He threw a scathing glance toward me, warning me by that look that he wasn't gonna go nowhere. Blood surged through my veins, sending a flash of heat over my whole body. Then I felt a calmness come over me as I realized what was going to happen.

My bullet smashed into his chest after his pistol had just cleared his holster.

He fell off the boardwalk and into the street. Doors started banging as people ran into the street, yelling, "Everything's gonna be alright. Black Patch is dead!" Folks started coming up to me, patting me on the back and shaking my hand.

"Who are you?" someone asked.

"My name is Jed Jenkins. My friends and me are here to visit my uncle. His name is James Seamus Jenkins. He owns a cattle ranch somewhere close to Velvet Sky."

"I know Mr. Jenkins," said an elderly gentleman.

"Is it possible, you could point us in the right direction?"

"Sure, take the right fork after you leave town, going west. About ten miles out, you'll see a gate with a sign on it. It says, Lazy Valley Ranch (JSJ)."

"Much obliged," I said. Then I turned and headed back to the livery stable.

CHAPTER TWENTY THREE

I told Half Loaf and Orville that, as soon as we had some breakfast, we would start out for my Uncle's ranch about ten miles west of town.

"We been jawing with Rufus here about this town, and we came to the conclusion that it ain't no different than all the other towns we passed through."

"Is there a good eating place in this town?"

"Yep, up the street one block, turn left, and there you are."

"Has it got a name?"

"It used to be called Fred's or something like that, but Fred died and some of his kin took it over. Never did change the name. The sign is so faded now you can't read it no how."

"Thank you. We'll see you in a bit. How about taking care of our animals?"

"Sure thing. See you in a bit."

After we ate, we paid Rufus, headed west out of town, then turned south. The terrain was up and down, with lots of greenery, grass, and trees. Ahead there were two of the tallest mountains I had ever seen. We crested a rise, and there in front of us was a large gate with a sign proclaiming, LAZY VALLEY RANCH. Under that, it said, JSJ.

Half Loaf said that was the brand they used on their cattle. Off in the distance, there were little black and brown specks. We found out later that they were cattle. Several hundred of them.

We rode for almost an hour. After passing a large horse corral, two large barns, a large bunkhouse, and various outbuildings, we saw a big, U-shaped Adobe, two-story house. It had a red tile roof, a covered porch, and was held up by wooden poles.

The porch ran the whole length of the front of the house. There was a brick courtyard, with lots of flower beds on all three sides. There was an Adobe wall surrounding the house and courtyards, and the entrance was a large iron gate.

Orville stopped the wagon and jumped down. "This here is some fine place," he proclaimed. "Is this your uncle's place?"

Half Loaf and me dismounted and tied our horses to the back of the wagon.

A bulky, dark-skinned, man came from our right side and asked, "Can I help you gentlemen?"

"We're looking for James Jenkins. Would this be his place?" I asked.

"Yes, this is his place. May I ask you what it is that you want? I'm the foreman, and we're not hiring right now. There will be work in the spring, though," he said.

"We aren't here looking for work. Mr. Jenkins is my uncle. My name is Jed Jenkins, and these are my friends,"

"Sure, I should have known, you with your red hair. Just like Mr. Jenkins."

"Is he here?" I asked.

"No, he is away on business, he and his whole family. He will return by the end of the week. But now you must come into the house and enjoy a cool drink after your long ride," he said.

We walked through the iron gate and past some flower beds. Just then, an oversized, carved, wooden door opened. A young Mexican woman waited just inside.

"My name is Rosita. Please, come in," she said. She was wearing a gray dress and white apron, and had her black hair tucked beneath a white ruffled cap.

"Come this way into the parlor," she said.

We followed Rosita, her heels bouncing off the tile floor. The room was large, and it had a stone fireplace in the center. There was a longhorn steer head above the mantle.

The furniture included a leather davenport, with matching chairs. Heavy, wooden beams crossed the ceiling. Indian rugs of bright red and turquoise hung on the walls. Beyond another archway was a dining room, with a large, polished, table that could easily seat ten people? Beyond the dining room, through another archway, was an office with a large desk and several filing cabinets. I assumed the bedrooms were upstairs.

"Please, be seated, I will bring refreshments," said Rosita. She returned with glasses and a big pitcher of lemonade, cool and sweet.

"Is there anything I can help you with until Mr. Jenkins returns? Since you are the nephew of Mr. Jenkins you may spend the night in the house, but your friends will have to stay in the bunkhouse."

"I'll stay in the bunkhouse with my friends

"As you wish," he said. "When you are finished with your lemonade, I will show you the way. Rosita will call you when supper is to be served."

We finished the lemonade, set the glasses on the tray, and said, "Lead the way."

The bunkhouse was a large, tall structure made of Adobe, with windows all the way around the walls. No matter which way the wind was blowing, it would blow through the bunkhouse. The foreman assigned us three bunks near the door where we entered.

We had brought our bed rolls, so we rolled them out on the bunks.

"These look a lot more comfortable than the back of the wagon, where I been sleeping."

The next morning, we walked to the pump next to a hand-dug well. Orville primed the pump, filled a bucket with fresh water, wet his bandanna and wiped his face, then filled a dipper and drank deeply.

"Um! That sure hits the spot early in the morning," he said.

Half Loaf filled the dipper and took a drink. "Yes, there is nothing as good as cool, fresh water from a well."

I filled the dipper and drank also. I dipped my bandanna into the bucket, wiped my forehead with the damp rag, and shaded my eyes against the bright sun.

Rosita called from the front porch, "Breakfast is ready, gentlemen. Please, come inside."

We went into the dining room and sat at the large table. It was a little intimidating sitting at such a big table, just the three of us.

Breakfast consisted of oatmeal, scrambled eggs, bacon, sausage, fried potatoes, buttered toast, fresh-squeezed orange juice, and milk. They sure did put on a big spread. I wondered if they ate like this all the time.

"I could get used to this ranching," said Orville. "This sure beats Army chow, a whole heap of a lot."

"Yes, it is a fine meal."

CHAPTER TWENTY FOUR

When we were finished eating, we stepped outside and were met by the foreman. "Perhaps, you would like to take a tour of the ranch?" he asked.

"That's just what we were planning to do."

Orville said, "I suppose I can ride Whitey, but I don't have a saddle. I traded my saddle when we upgraded the buckboard, remember?"

"That is not a problem, we have many saddles."

We saddled the horses and joined the foreman in front of the barn.

"What would you like to see first?" he asked.

"I always wanted to see some roping and branding," Orville said.

"They're branding in the south forty today. We'll join 'em there," the foreman said. "This way, please."

We rode for half an hour at a pretty fast clip. As we crossed over a little rise, we saw hundreds of cattle.

There was a fire off to the side, with half a dozen cowboys. Two of the men were roping and hog-tying a young cow. Another was heating a branding iron in the fire. As soon as the men had the cow secured, the one with the branding iron held the hot iron against the cow's back hip. The smell of burning hair and flesh was rancid.

"Kind of smells like the battlefield," said Orville.

"How many cattle do you have here on the ranch?"

He answered, "At last count, there was 752, and that's not counting the calves."

"How many acres is the ranch?" I asked.

"Many acres of deeded land, and thousands of acres of free range. The entire ranch includes 260 square miles. I think that is a little over 166,000 acres. We have twenty cowhands riding for us, and we hire fifteen more, during the busiest season. We stay very busy all year round.

"There are ten windmills spread around the range in strategic areas. We have one man whose only job is keeping all the windmills up and running. We have one other man for all the repair work that needs to be done around the ranch. The cattle always have water, even in the slow rainy season. There's a large lake located in the lower part of the range. We have 400 acres dedicated to growing wheat for feed during the hard winters," he said. "There is a large vegetable garden located behind the main house, and we grow enough vegetables that we sell part of them in town at the general store. It is one of the largest ranches in all of Arizona Territories."

"I wish Pa could be here to see what his brother has accomplished. He would be so proud," I said.

"Thank you for showing us around. Now I believe I would like to ride alone for a while," I said.

They said they would meet me back at the main house when I returned.

The landscape was so much different than Texas. Now, don't misunderstand me, I'm a Texan, through and through. I didn't say I liked it more, just different.

As I rode, I asked myself, *could this maybe be a place where I could settle down, maybe raise a family*? Somehow, I didn't think that was going to happen. I felt the Lord wanted me to keep traveling the country, helping those that needed help, and ridding the land of the evil men that preyed on innocent folks. Was that what He wanted me to do?

CHAPTER TWENTY FIVE

I rode back to the ranch house, and Half Loaf was waiting for me as I entered the yard.

"The foreman said he received a telegram from Mr. Jenkins. He and his family will be arriving in two days."

"That sounds real good. I'm looking forward to meeting them. I don't even know if my cousins are male or female."

"Perhaps there will be a girl about my age."

"Do you really want a girlfriend? What with all the traveling we have to do?"

"I suppose not. However, who says she has to be a permanent girlfriend?"

"I guess you have a point." We went back to the bunkhouse to wait for supper.

About twenty minutes went by, then Rosita came to the door of the main house and hollered, "Supper is ready, come and get it."

We washed up and headed for the house to eat supper. The table was, as usual, filled with delicious food. Roast beef, candied yams, corn on the cob, boiled potatoes, bread and butter, with a large pitcher of lemonade.

"I sure could get used to this," Orville said.

"Me also," said Half Loaf.

"Yes, it is a very good meal."

We finished with the meal, then went into the kitchen to tell the cook how much we enjoyed her cooking. Afterward, we walked outside and sat looking at the sky. The orange tint of the moon was almost shut out from the dark clouds.

"Looks like it's gonna come a gully washer," said Orville.

"Well rain is always needed on a cattle ranch." I answered.

"Let's git inside before we git wet," said Orville.

We went inside and crawled into our bunks.

The next morning after breakfast we went for a short walk around the main house. We walked behind the barn and saw a group of men standing around the corral. They were jumping up and hollering.

There in the corral was a young man riding a bucking horse.

"He is making it look easy," said Half Loaf. "I know that it is indeed not as easy as he makes it look."

"That young man is Randy Brockman. He is the best bronc-buster in four countries, and he is only twenty-two years old," said one of the men standing there. "We can't have a rowdy horse around the cattle when we're rounding them up.

"Randy's a top wrangler and could work any spread he wanted. Many others have offered him higher wages, but he will only work for Mr. Jenkins. Course it might be 'cause he's the father of Miss Laura Mae Jenkins. She sure is a looker, but she only has eyes for the banker's son, Thad Newcomb. Randy don't like it much, but he says his turn'll come. You can take odds on it."

"I reckon if we're gonna go look at this here ranch, I'd better go ask the foreman if I can borrow that blame saddle again. I'll meet you fellows back at the bunkhouse, in say fifteen minutes or so."

We met with Orville and the foreman at the bunkhouse.

"I understand you want to tour the ranch again. Is that so?"

"Yes, but if you don't mind, we would like to go alone."

"That will be fine. See that you do not get lost."

After a couple hours, Orville said, "I reckon we could look for a week and still not see all of this ranch."

"Yes, it is a big spread. At one time I dreamed of owning a spread like this."

"It's not too late, maybe your uncle will let you have a section of this one."

"I think God may have other plans for me."

"How can you be so sure what God wants you to do?"

"I talk with Him and He lets me know."

"You mean God talks to you, just like we're talking now?"

"Not exactly like that, but I have no doubt when He wants me to know something."

"I never was much on this God stuff. I seen too much bad stuff during the war."

"But you made it through, didn't you? Don't you think maybe God had a hand in that?"

"Maybe, I'll have to think on that for a while. I'd have to say thank you if'en He did have a part in me gittin back."

"He's always waiting to hear from you, anytime, day or night. Give it a try sometime."

"Maybe."

"I talk to God all the time," Half Loaf said. "It gives me a good feeling on the inside. Jed introduced Him to me one night not so long ago. Perhaps if you accepted

Him into your heart like I did, it would be easier for you to talk to Him."

"Maybe. This sure is pretty country, ain't it. I reckon you're gonna tell me God made all this."

"I think you know the answer to that question."

CHAPTER TWENTY SIX

We rode until noon, then stopped at a pond. "If it wasn't so cold, I could stand a bath," I commented.

"Some folks take a bath even when it's cold," Half Loaf replied.

"But not in a pond in the winter time," said Orville.

"I think I'm going to do it anyway," I said.

"Jed, you'll freeze yer you know what," said Orville.

"What the heck. I got a fresh change in my saddle bags. I can dry off with my dirty ones."

"That's another reason I can't do it. I ain't got no change of clothes."

"I do, and I will go with you, Jed," said Half Loaf.

"Young pups ain't got a lick of sense. Go ahead. You'll probably ketch pneumonia, and I ain't gonna take care of you when you do."

Half Loaf and myself tethered our mounts to a little bush over by the pond. Then we both took our fresh clothes out of our saddlebags and walked over to the edge of the pond.

"Last one in is a rotten egg." I removed my clothes and waded into the freezing cold water.

Half Loaf was right behind me. I looked at him and he looked at me. We were both shivering so bad we couldn't say anything. Again, he looked at me and I looked at him. We both nodded our heads and headed for the bank. What we didn't realize was, while we were in the water, Orville had taken our clothes. Both the clean and the dirty.

Half Loaf started saying something in Spanish.

"I don't know what you're saying, but I don't think it's anything nice."

"I'm sorry, Jed, but I am so angry."

"I know. So am I, but we have to forgive an ignoramus like Orville."

"What are you calling me, you young whippersnapper?"

"You really need to give our clothes back, before we catch a chill."

We were both standing there in our birthday suits, when I looked over the pond and saw a dust cloud. Someone was coming.

"Come on Orville, there's someone coming. I would sure like to be dressed to greet them."

"Oh, alright. Can't have no fun at all with little boys." He went over to a clump of bushes and retrieved our clothes.

There wasn't any need to dry off as the air had gotten us completely dry. However, we were covered with goosebumps.

"You fellows know I was jest playing, don't you? You do know I love you both."

"Sure, Orville. And we love you, but I wouldn't be surprised if sometime, when you aren't expecting it, we get even."

"Aw, shucks, I didn't think about that."

"Who you reckon is coming in such a rush?" asked Orville.

"I reckon we'll know soon enough." I answered.

The foreman rode up and stepped down. "I wasn't sure where you would be. I sure didn't figure on you going swimming, at least not this time of year. Why didn't you use the bathtub in the house? It would definitely have been more comfortable than the pond. There was a fellow came asking for you to come to town."

"Did they say why I was needed in town?"

"Nope, just that they wanted you to come."

"Well, I reckon I'll go see what they want. You fellows want to go to town?"

"Is it alright to ride this saddle to town?" Orville asked the foreman.

"Absolutely, the saddle is yours as long as you are guests of the ranch."

"Yes, we'll go along." I told him.

"Let's fill our canteens here and ride for town," said Orville.

CHAPTER TWENTY SEVEN

We rode into town and went to the livery stable. If anyone knew what I was wanted for, it would be Rufus.

"Step down, fellows. I figured you'd stop here before you went to see the town council."

"You have any idea what they want to see me about?"

"I reckon they'll offer you a job. They know you've turned down the job as sheriff before. I think they are gonna offer you something a little different."

"Where is this town council right now?"

"They're probably over at the hotel. We don't have any other place for important meetings, not since the town burned down about five years back."

"Alright then, do you fellows want to go with me?"

"I don't reckon they want to see us. Jest you, I would imagine," said Orville.

"Alright, I'll see you later."

I walked down Main Street to the Bronson Hotel. There were four men inside, two pacing, two seated.

"Hello, gentlemen, you wanted to see me?"

"Yes, Mr. Jenkins. We want very much to meet with you about something of utmost importance. Please have a seat."

I took the spot across from the two men who were seated. "What can I do for you gentlemen?"

"We have a proposition for you. We know that you turned down the job of being the sheriff, but we think we have something that would suit you much better than being a sheriff."

"And what might that be?"

"We want you to be our peacekeeper."

"Isn't that just a sheriff with a different name?"

"Oh no, we just want you to take care of troublemakers that arrive in town. You won't have to arrest drunks or anybody like that. Just the ones who come into town wanting to cause trouble."

"Like I said, sheriff with a different name. I'm not interested."

"Perhaps if you heard the salary you might consider it?"

"I only use my gun at times of people needing help. Now if I'm here when one of these troublemakers comes to town, I will be glad to help out. But no, I'm not available for your peacekeeper job. Thank you, but no thank you."

I went back to the livery stable and told them what the council wanted.

"Are we gonna have this offered at every town we pass through? You know, it might not be so bad, it could be a steady job. No more traveling around."

"I don't feel that's what God wants me to do."

"Alright, if you say so. I reckon me and Half Loaf will be at your side no matter what."

"I really appreciate that. Thanks."

Now let's go back to the ranch for more of that good chow.

CHAPTER TWENTY EIGHT

We arrived back at the ranch just in time for supper.

Rosita said, "I thought I was going to have to throw it out to the hogs."

"You should know I ain't gonna miss one of cook's fine meals."

We moseyed around the ranch for two days. I was very anxious to meet my uncle.

Pa had talked about all his brothers a lot. He was real sorry about the way they had parted ways. He always wanted to visit with each one, but it never happened.

I woke before everyone else, so I went in the house and took advantage of the bathtub. It was indeed much better than the pond. I changed into clean clothes, combed my hair, and went in to eat breakfast. I was early, so I sat at the table.

Rosita came in and asked, "What are you doing here so early, Jed?"

"I took a bath so I would be fresh to meet my uncle."

"Maybe you're a little nervous, yes? Breakfast will be just a few minutes.

Would you like some coffee while you wait?"

"Yes, thank you, Rosita."

She returned with a cup and a pot of hot coffee.

"Thank you," I said, as she poured a cup for me.

"You can pour the next one yourself."

I waited about ten minutes and Rosita served breakfast.

"Hey, was you gonna eat without us?" Orville asked as he and Half Loaf came into the dining room.

"You both know I love you, but when it comes to food, it's not much of a race."

"Your uncle, he is coming today?" asked Half Loaf.

"That's what the telegram said." I answered.

"I bet you are excited, yes?" Half Loaf asked.

"He is also very nervous," Rosita said as she was passing through.

"Nothing to be nervous about, he's kinfolk," said Orville.

"I've never seen or met him, nor he me," I said.

"He'll see your red hair and know you're his kin," Orville said.

"Thank you all for that encouragement," I said.

"I think I'll go out to the corral and talk to Randy for a little while. As always, Rosita, the meal was fantastic. Please convey my gratitude to the cook."

I told the fellows goodbye and left to go to the corral. Randy and a couple of men were getting a horse ready to ride. Randy was whispering in the horse's ear, and you could tell it was having a calming effect on him. I find it amazing how some men can be so gentle with animals, while others are downright mean.

I could see Randy was going to be busy for a while, so I climbed up on the corral fence to watch.

Randy had finished talking to the horse and was putting the saddle on him. He was almost finished; I could tell by the way the horse started prancing back and forth around the corral. Randy would turn him one direction, then the other.

Just then I heard a carriage pulling into the front yard.

CHAPTER TWENTY NINE

I rushed around the barn just as the folks started unloading. I spotted my uncle first. There was no way to mistake him for anyone else, what with his red hair; it was almost the same color as Pa's. He finished helping the women down from the carriage, then he looked my way. He seemed to freeze in his tracks. He turned to the women and said something, and they all looked my direction.

He started walking toward me. "They told me in town that someone was waiting, but I had no idea. And who might you be, young man? Have we met before?"

"No, sir. We haven't met. But I do know who you are, and I've been wanting to meet you for a very long time. My name is Jedidiah Isaiah Jenkins, and I believe you're my uncle."

"Jedidiah Isaiah Jenkins. I believe I have heard that name before. How's your pa?"

"Pa's dead. He was killed over a month ago."

"Oh, Jedidiah, I'm so sorry. You came all the way from Texas by yourself?"

"No, I have some very good friends with me."

"Let's go in the house and we can do some getting acquainted. I want you to meet your aunt, and your cousins."

We went in the house.

"Come into the living room. May I call you Jed?"

"I prefer Jed, sir."

"Let me go upstairs and freshen up a bit, then we we'll visit. Please sit. Here, in this chair. It is the most comfortable one."

I was sitting in the big chair when a young girl with hair the color of her father's came in. "Who are you? You have hair the same as Papa and me."

"My name is Jed, and the reason my hair's the same as you is because we're cousins."

"I didn't know I had any cousins. Are you the only one?"

"I'm probably the only one from Texas. I don't know if you have others somewhere else. What's your name?"

"It's Jennifer. Will you be staying here long?'

"I can't really answer that question, because I don't know when or if I'll have to leave."

"I hope you can stay a long time. I have to go now. It was nice meeting you, Jed."

My uncle and me had a very nice time getting acquainted. He couldn't understand what I was doing traveling around the country and getting into gunfights. He showed me around the ranch, and to some special places that only he knew about. He introduced me to the rest of my cousins and my aunt, and he told me how he had battled Indians, floods, droughts, rustlers, and cattle fever. A few years back, he had lost over half the cattle. Back in '60 he had to completely rebuild the house and barn when they burned down. He said it was almost like starting all over again. "But here we are, very successful."

CHAPTER THIRTY

One day when we were riding back from one of the special places, he asked me if I would consider staying on a spell, so I could get to know the whole family better.

"I tried again to explain to him that I had to do what God wanted me to do."

"Don't you think God might want you to live with family?"

"I'll pray about it." And I did just that while riding back to what could be a home for me.

When we rode into the yard back at the ranch house, Half Loaf was waiting for me. "There is a telegram for you, Jed." He gave it to me.

Who would be sending me a telegram? I wondered as I ripped it open. It read: You are needed in Angry Orchard, Colorado Territory. There is a group of four men terrorizing our town. We heard about you from my brother in Windy Butte, New Mexico Territory. He said, that you had helped them with a similar problem. We are willing to compensate you for your time if you would be willing to help us. Please, if you can, come at once. Cordially yours, C.D. Watkins, Mayor.

"I guess I know now what I'm supposed to do with my life." *Thank you, Lord, for letting me know so quickly.*

I would like to have stayed and visited some more, but I was needed elsewhere. I tried to explain to my uncle that God guides me on the path as I travel the land, helping those that need help.

"I don't really understand, but I do except that you are your own man and you have to do what you feel in your heart. Here it is, you just arrived, we just gotten to know one another, and now you're already leaving."

"Thank you for understanding. Now if I could ask you for one more thing. I don't really care for long goodbyes, so could you please explain to your family I had to leave suddenly? Tell them how much I enjoyed meeting and visiting with each of them."

"I can do that for you, and remember you'll be in our prayers, always. And if you're ever back this way, you'd better come visit. Goodbye, Jed, travel safe."

"Thank you, sir. May God bless you and yours."

I rounded up Orville and Half Loaf, told them about the telegram, and that I felt this is something God wants me to do. I wasn't asking them to follow me, but if they wanted to, they were more than welcome.

"You think you can get rid of us that easy?" said Orville.

Half Loaf said, "I agree. I will follow you wherever you want to go."

"Let's get a good night's rest, tomorrow we go to Angry Orchard, Colorado Territory."

Look for the continuing adventures of The Traveler. Next exciting chapter in the lives of Jed, Orville and Half Loaf and a new character is joining the crew in

Angry Orchard, Colorado

Coming soon.

www.ingramcontent.com/pod-product-compliance
Lightning Source LLC
Chambersburg PA
CBHW050745180726
48003CB00020B/1873